The Two Runaways

A WOODLAND MYSTERY

By Irene Schultz

To Lil Shepard and my other dear teacher friends who encouraged and helped me

The Woodland Mysteries™

The Two Runaways
©1996 Story by Irene Schultz
Cover and illustrations by Taylor Bruce
Map illustration by Alicia Kramer
©1996 Wright Group Publishing, Inc.

The Woodland Mysteries were created by the
Wright Group development team.

The Wright Group
19201 120th Avenue NE
Bothell, WA 98011

Printed in the United States of America

10 9 8 7 6 5 4 3

ISBN: 0-7802-7243-9

What family solves mysteries...has adventures all over the world...and loves oatmeal cookies?

It's the Woodlanders!

Sammy Westburg (10 years old)
His sister Kathy Westburg (13)
His brother Bill Westburg (14)
His best friend Dave Briggs (16)
His best grown-up friend Mrs. Tandy
And Mop, their little dog!

The children all lost their parents, but with Mrs. Tandy have made their own family.

Why are they called the Woodlanders? Because they live in a big house in the Bluff Lake woods. On Woodland Street!

Together they find fun, mystery, and adventure. What are they up to now?

Read on!

Meet the Woodlanders!

Sammy Westburg
Sammy is a ten-year-old wonder! He's big for his fifth-grade class, and big-mouthed, too. He has wild hair and makes awful spider faces. Even so, you can't help liking him.

Bill Westburg
Bill, fourteen, is friendly and strong, and only one inch taller than his brother Sammy. He loves Sammy, but pokes him to make him be quiet! He's in junior high.

Kathy Westburg
Kathy, thirteen, is small, shy, and smart. She wants to be a doctor someday! She loves to be with Dave, and her brothers kid her about it. She's in junior high, too.

Dave Briggs

Dave, sixteen, is tall and blond. He can't walk, so he uses a wheelchair and drives a special car. He likes coaching high-school sports, solving mysteries, and reading. And Kathy!

Mrs. Tandy

Sometimes the kids call her Mrs. T. She's Becky Tandy, their tall, thin, caring friend. She's always ready for a new adventure, and for making cookies!

Mop

Mop is the family's little tan dog. Sometimes they have to leave him behind with friends. But he'd much rather be running after Sammy.

Table of Contents

Chapter 1: A Fight at School

One morning before school, Sammy Westburg stood on the playground.

He was talking with some other fifth-graders.

All of a sudden an older boy ran up to them.

He shouted, "Hey, Sammy! Your brother's in a fight over at the junior high! Come on!"

Sammy raced across the playground. A ring of kids were watching the fight, yelling.

Sammy saw his fourteen-year-old brother Bill in the middle of the crowd.

He was trying to push a taller boy away from him.

Bill was short and chubby, but strong. The other boy was much taller, but thin. He was hitting Bill's chest.

Bill yelled, "Come off it, Mark! Get away from me!"

The tall boy said, "I'm going to mash you, you fat little toad."

Bill said, "You and who else, you skinny tree frog?" He ducked under the tall boy's arms and pushed him hard.

The boy almost fell.

Bill said, "Now leave me alone!" and walked away.

But the tall boy started to run after him.

The kids were all afraid he'd get Bill from behind. They yelled, "Watch out! Watch out, Bill!"

Just then, Sammy ran toward the tall boy from the side. He butted him in the stomach, like a goat.

The boy fell to the ground.

Sammy yelled, "You leave my brother alone, you creep!"

He shook his fist.

His hair was sticking out all over.

Then the first bell rang.

Bill ran over to Sammy and patted him on the back. He said, "Thanks, pal. See you after school. It's a half-day today, you know!"

Sammy said, "Believe me, I know! See you later!"

Then Bill went to class. He sat down just before the last bell.

Mark was already in his desk, in the next row, one seat back. He leaned over to Bill and whispered, "I'll see YOU after school."

Bill tried to look calm, but inside he felt wild.

He was thinking, "Why did Mark start

a fight? Does he have something against black people or what?

"I've never said anything mean to him. In fact I always felt sorry for him. He's always by himself ..."

Bill heard the teacher's voice saying, "Well, what's your answer, Bill?"

He jumped. He was so upset, he hadn't even heard the question.

He said, "What did you ask, Mrs. Santos?"

Mrs. Santos said, "Bill, I'm not going to say it again. I've asked you twice now."

She looked around the classroom. She said, "Mark, do you know the answer?"

The tall boy shook his head.

Mrs. Santos looked at them both, hard. She said, "You two might think about studying before school, instead of wasting time."

She called on someone else who said,

"Florida is where that moon rocket took off."

Bill groaned inside. He thought, "I knew THAT! If only I'd been listening. And why did she call on me and Mark? Does she know about the fight?"

When the bell rang, Bill was worried that Mark would come after him again.

But Mark was nowhere around.

Bill's sister Kathy ran up to him and hugged him.

He said, "Hey, Kathy, let me up for air!"

Thirteen-year-old Kathy blushed red.

She said, "Bill, are you OK? I heard you were in a fight!

"First I heard you had a red mark on your face.

"Then I heard you had a black eye.

"Then I heard you needed stitches in your head!

"My teacher checked for me and said you were all right, but I was still worried."

Just then Sammy ran over from the grade school.

He said, "Hi, Bill, you toad! That's not a bad name that frog boy gave you."

Bill didn't get mad at Sammy this time. He just slapped his arm around Sammy's shoulders and walked along with him and Kathy.

He said, "Thanks for saving me this morning, old goat."

Sammy bragged, "You should have seen me butt that guy, Kathy. He FLEW through the air! ZOOOOM!"

Kathy asked, "What started the fight? Is it over now?"

Sammy looked worried. He said, "I sure hope so. Because they could kick Bill out of school if this keeps up."

Bill said, "That's just the problem. I don't know what started it. I don't really know the guy ... he's only been here for two weeks. I've never even talked to him before today, except to say hi."

They turned up the path to their house in the woods.

Mrs. Tandy stood outside waving to them. She said, "I just took our lunch to the clubhouse!"

Mrs. Tandy lived with Bill, Kathy, and Sammy Westburg, and their sixteen-year-old friend Dave Briggs.

The five of them called themselves the Woodlanders.

They all loved the clubhouse.

It was the size of a very small garage, with tables, chairs, and a stove in it.

There were even shelves for dishes, flashlights, and writing things. It was like a little home.

When they sat down to lunch, Sammy said, "Hey, Bill, tell Mrs. Tandy the whole awful story!"

After Mrs. Tandy heard it all, she said, "Well, my lands! What in the world made that boy act like that?"

Bill said, "I wish I knew. I thought he'd be waiting to fight me after school."

Kathy said, "Do you really think he would try to get you again?"

Bill said, "Who knows. Anyway, we need to get to the store. Let's go."

He got up and walked out into the yard. The others joined him.

Sammy said, "That was a good lunch. What should we make for dinner?"

Kathy said, "How about cheeseburgers with tomato slices on them?"

Sammy said, "Cheeseburgers! I think I'm hungry again. Right now! Feed me now, or I'll die. Don't make me go to the store!"

He wrapped his arms and legs around a tree.

Everyone was laughing and trying to pull him away.

Mrs. Tandy poked him and said, "Get

along there, you tree frog!"

Sammy said, "Tree frog! Hey! That's just what Bill called that boy!"

He started jumping and croaking like a frog.

He hopped right down the path in the woods to the sidewalk.

Then Bill said quietly, "Oh my gosh. Look!"

There stood the tall boy, leaning against a tree on the edge of their yard.

His skinny arms and legs looked a lot like the thin branches around him.

He looked at them with a funny smile and said, "So THIS is where you live."

Then he stuck his hands in his pockets, gave a little laugh, and walked off.

Kathy said, "Oh, no! Do you think Mark saw Sammy and thinks he was making fun of him?"

Sammy said, "I don't care if he did."

Bill said, "Come on, Sammy. We don't have to be mean just because he was."

Mrs. Tandy said, "Maybe he came here to say he was sorry. After all, he didn't try to fight Bill after school."

Bill said, "Well, I have a feeling this isn't over yet. But all we can do is wait and see."

Chapter 2: A Noise in the Dark

Dave got home from high school later that afternoon.

The Woodlanders ran to meet him, along with their little dog Mop.

As they headed into the kitchen, Bill told Dave about the fight.

Dave said, "Bill, this guy sounds pretty strange. You'll have to keep an eye on him."

Sammy said, "Something's eating him, that's for sure."

Mrs. Tandy said, "Well, how about if WE eat THESE?" She put down a tray of oatmeal cookies.

They spent the afternoon at the clubhouse. They were building a fireplace so they could take out the stove.

They had cut a big hole in one wall.

They laid bricks outside of it for the back and sides of the fireplace.

Dave said, "Let's do the chimney tomorrow. I'll close up the opening with this." He put a piece of plywood over the hole.

Sammy shouted, "Come on!" He

grabbed Dave's wheelchair and rushed him to the house. "Remember those cheeseburgers!"

In a second he had Dave inside.

After dinner and homework, everyone was ready for bed.

In the middle of the night, Kathy woke up suddenly.

She heard a noise.

She listened for it again. Nothing.

She said to herself, "That old raccoon must be trying to get into the garbage cans."

She went back to sleep.

In a few minutes she woke up again. The noise was louder this time.

It didn't sound like garbage cans.

It sounded more like rocks bumping each other.

Kathy got up. She saw that Sammy's

door was open.

She sneaked over to his room. She said, "Sammy! Sammy, wake up! Something's making a weird noise in the backyard!"

Sammy groaned under his covers, "Let me sleep ... go away."

She said, "Sammy, wake up! I'm scared!" She shook him.

Sammy shouted, "WHAT IS IT!"

He was awful when he was half-asleep. He threw the covers off of his head.

Kathy said, "I think I hear an animal out near the clubhouse."

Sammy said, "Don't be silly! If something were over there, Mop would be barking his head off!"

Just then they BOTH heard the noise.

CLINK ... CLINK.

Mop ran out of the closet where he had been sleeping.

He started barking his head off.

Sammy hopped out of bed in his shorts.

He said, "Kathy! Something's out there! Why didn't you wake me up?"

Kathy said, "Don't turn on any lights until we wake up the others."

They flew across the hall to Mrs. Tandy's room. She was already coming out in her robe and slippers.

Kathy said, "Something's out by the clubhouse!"

CLINK ... CLINK ... CLINK.

They heard it again.

Mrs. Tandy whispered, "Don't do anything yet. I'll go get Bill and Dave."

She sneaked to the other end of the house, to the big bedroom where they slept.

She said, "Boys, wake up. There's something strange going on outside."

Dave got himself into his wheelchair, quick as a flash.

He and Bill and Mrs. Tandy raced to the kitchen. Everyone went to a window. They all had flashlights.

Bill whispered, "Wait until we hear it again. Then I'll yell 'NOW!' and we can all shine our lights!"

Dave whispered, "Ready."

They waited. They were hardly breathing.

All of a sudden they heard CLINK!

CLINK! CLINK! CLINK! CLINK!

"Now!" Bill shouted.

On went the flashlights and the porch light.

They dashed outside.

But they were too late. They saw something move in the bushes near the clubhouse. Then it was gone.

And then they saw only loose bricks, right where their new fireplace had been.

Their new walls were a mess!

Kathy said, "Oh, no! Ruined!"

Sammy said, "After all our work! I'm going to set a box trap for that stinker raccoon."

Bill said, "Wow. We work on it for hours, and a stupid raccoon spoils it in minutes."

Mrs. Tandy said, "I don't think it was a raccoon. Raccoons go after food ... and there wasn't any food in the club-house.

"I've never heard of one just tearing a wall down."

Dave said, "Maybe it pushed the ply-wood off by accident. So it just climbed inside the walls to look around.

"Then it got scared and pushed its way out instead of climbing out."

Sammy said, "What if it was a BEAR! Where will I get a bear trap?" He went to the back door of the clubhouse.

Dave said, "Don't open the door!

"Let's not take any chances on what might be inside. Let's get some help."

Mrs. Tandy said, "I'll call Chief Hemster and see if he's at the police station."

Sammy teased, "Sure! Any excuse to call your BOYfriend, Mrs. T.!"

They went back inside.

Kathy turned on some lights in the house.

Sammy ran for his bathrobe. Then he made hot chocolate while they waited.

Minutes later their good friend Chief Hemster drove up.

They told him what had happened.

He said, "Stay behind me. Let's take a look."

They all walked back outside and over to the clubhouse.

They looked for signs of an animal ... paw prints, scratch marks, fur. They didn't find a thing.

But then Dave shined his light on the ground near the bushes.

He said, "Hey! Take a look at this!"

Sammy said, "Holy cats!"

On the ground was a big blue shoe.

Chapter 3: The Big Blue Shoe

Mrs. Tandy said, "Well, I'll be. I never saw a bear that wore sneakers!"

Chief Hemster said, "I didn't THINK it was an animal that tore down your wall.

Now, who would do a mean thing like this?"

The Woodlanders looked at each other. They knew exactly who it might be.

But at first no one spoke up. Not even Sammy, who had trouble keeping quiet about anything.

Bill and Kathy picked up the plywood. They leaned it against the fireplace opening.

They went back to the house to drink their hot chocolate.

Chief Hemster looked into the shoe. He said, "Well, this is a size twelve. It belongs to someone pretty tall, I bet. Wonder who it is."

Sammy poked Bill under the table.

Then Bill said, "Chief, we know who it could be. His name is Mark Witt.

"But he's a new kid in town. We don't want to make trouble for him with the police."

Chief Hemster said, "Looks like he might have made his own trouble."

Sammy said, "He picked a fight with Bill this morning and I butted him down to the ground."

Sammy pounded his chest like Tarzan.

Mrs. Tandy said, "If it WAS this boy Mark, why was he running around here alone in the middle of the night? Wouldn't his family wonder where he was?"

Bill said, "It's funny. This morning I almost hated him. But now I feel even more sorry for him than I did before.

"I don't want to make things worse for him."

Kathy said, "But what if he comes back and wrecks something else? Or hurts you?"

Chief Hemster said, "I don't think he'd take that big a risk. But he might come back for his shoe."

The chief had been looking at the shoe carefully. He said, "This is tied tight. How do you think it came off?"

Sammy said, "If you ever saw him, you'd know how. His body is as thin as my leg. His arms look like sticks, almost.

"That's why Bill called him a skinny tree frog, after he called Bill a fat little toad."

Bill said, "I bet his skinny foot just

slipped out when he was running."

Mrs. Tandy said, "Well, I was thinking I'd like to shake that boy. But if he's that thin, I'd like to feed him instead."

Dave said, "Look, Chief. Maybe you can help us find out what his problem is. Then we can help him before he gets into worse trouble.

"Maybe Mrs. Tandy can call his parents tomorrow, and we can meet with them and Mark."

Chief Hemster said, "That's a good idea. I'll stay out of it unless you need me. Well, I'll be on my way. Thanks for the hot chocolate!"

Early the next day Mrs. Tandy got Mark's number from the school's brand-new phone book.

When she called, a friendly voice answered, "Lake-Side Home."

Mrs. Tandy said, "LAKE-SIDE HOME! Is this the home for runaway boys from the city?"

The voice said, "That's right!"

Mrs. Tandy said, "Why, you sound just like Ann Strong! This is Becky Tandy. Is that you, Ann?"

Mrs. Strong said, "Hi, Becky! It IS me. I help out here every morning. How can I help you, my friend?"

Mrs. Tandy said, "Bill got into a fight with a boy named Mark Witt. Does he live there?"

Mrs. Strong said, "Mark Witt? Are you sure? Yes, he lives here, but ... poor kid ... he's in bad trouble."

Mrs. Tandy said, "My goodness! Did he try to hurt somebody there?"

Mrs. Strong said, "No, no, Becky. He's a very fine boy. That's why I'm so surprised to hear about this fight."

Mrs. Tandy said, "Well, can we get together with you to talk about this?"

Mrs. Strong said, "Of course. How's after school today?"

Later that morning, when Bill and Kathy got to the junior high, Mark was nowhere in sight.

In fact, he wasn't in school at all.

At lunchtime Kathy called Mrs. Tandy. She said, "Mark's not here today. Maybe, if that WAS him last night, he got hurt somehow."

Mrs. Tandy was surprised. She said, "That's funny, Kathy. When I called his number today, I found out that he's living at the boys' home.

"I talked to Ann Strong. She knows him well. She didn't say one word about Mark not going to school today."

She told Kathy about the meeting they had planned.

After school, Bill, Kathy, and Sammy walked home together. They saw Mrs. Strong's car in their driveway.

But something was wrong. Chief Hemster's car was there, too.

They ran inside.

Sammy said, "Hey, what happened? Where's Mark?"

Chief Hemster said only one word. "Missing."

Chapter 4: Where's Mark?

Just then they heard the back door slam.

Dave was back early from school.

He wheeled into the living room ... then looked around at the worried faces.

He said, "What's up?"

Mrs. Tandy said, "Nobody knows where Mark is. He disappeared from the Lake-Side Home.

"That's where he lives. I found out today that Ann Strong works there! She knows him!"

Sammy said, "I can't believe he's MISSING! Maybe it's my fault that he ran off. Like Kathy said.

"Maybe he did think I was making fun of him yesterday."

Bill said, "No, Sammy. It's not your fault. My whole class could have been nicer to him."

Dave said, "So, Mrs. Strong, do you have ANY idea where Mark might be?"

Mrs. Strong said, "Well, at breakfast he told me he'd hurt himself.

"He had on one shoe and one slipper. He said wearing his other shoe hurt his foot, and he'd have to go to school like that.

"He left with the other boys. But by the time they got to school, I guess he was long gone.

"I'm so worried I could cry." A tear ran down her cheek.

Dave said, "Wait a minute. I know why Mark didn't go to school. And it isn't because he hurt his foot!"

He wheeled out to the kitchen and came back with the blue shoe.

He said, "How many pairs of shoes does Mark have, Mrs. Strong?"

She wiped her eyes. "Just one. Some blue gym shoes. Dr. Strong and I were going to take him out this weekend to buy—"

Then she said, "My word! Is that Mark's shoe?"

Dave said, "It must be. He must

have lost it here last night. I'll bet he didn't want to show up at school wearing only one shoe."

Mrs. Strong said, "Then he might not be hurt? Oh, thank goodness!"

Chief Hemster said, "Well, we have to find this boy. The plain truth is, we don't know where to start to look.

"He may be here, or he may be back in the city with millions of other people.

"Ann, suppose you tell us what you can about Mark. It might help us find him."

She answered, "Well, usually I wouldn't just blab anyone's secrets. But Mark needs help, so it seems right to tell you.

"And maybe then you'll see why Dr. Strong and I feel he's such a fine boy. We may even try to adopt him."

Mrs. Strong told this story:

"Mark has lived in foster homes for as long as he can remember.

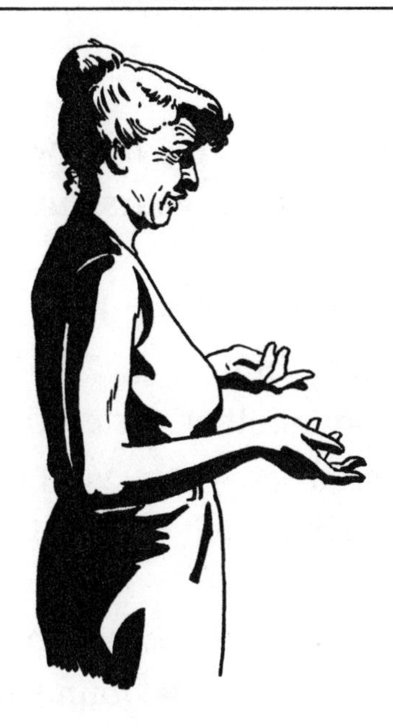

"In his first eight years, he was with ten different families.

"Each family sent him away.

"Maybe they wanted only small children.

"Or they gave birth to a baby of their own.

"Or they moved away and couldn't take a foster child with them, because of state rules.

"The best home he had was the one he was in for four years, until he was twelve.

"He felt they loved him and were going to adopt him.

"They had another foster child named Kelly Evans, three years younger. Mark and Kelly loved each other, like brother and sister.

"Then about two years ago, the foster father lost his job. He found a new job in Texas. He had to leave Mark and Kelly behind.

"No one wanted both kids together after that.

"So they were placed in two homes, a hundred miles apart.

"They were terribly lonely for each other.

"In a few weeks, Mark got a letter from Kelly. It said her foster parents were mean to her.

"They hit her when she made mistakes. They didn't give her much food.

"She was going to run away.

"Mark knew Kelly would try to find him. And he knew she would be sent back if she turned up where he lived.

"So he packed a few things in a brown bag. He watched for her.

"Late one night he spotted Kelly across the street. He sneaked out and ran away with her.

"He and Kelly hid out in the city.

"At first they lived outside. On cold nights, they put on all their clothes and slept under porches.

"They asked for work at stores and houses every day.

"They swept sidewalks.

"They cleaned basements.

"They ran errands.

"That's how they made money to buy food.

"Sometimes they couldn't earn money. They had to look for food in garbage cans.

"Soon it got too cold to sleep outside. One day Mark saw an old apartment house.

"It looked empty, but there was a small light in one room.

"The kids tapped on the door.

"An old man opened it. When he saw the two cold children, he let them use a room near his, from that night on.

"For nearly two years, Mark took care of Kelly the best he was able.

"Through all this, Mark worried about Kelly missing school.

"So he took her to a library every day to read with her. He showed her all the math he knew.

"But one day, about four months ago, Kelly cut her foot on some glass. It became red and swollen.

"It got worse and worse.

"At last Mark HAD to take Kelly into a hospital.

"Mark was sent to a foster home again. When Kelly got better, she was sent to another one.

"No one told Mark where she was.

"Mark kept running away to try to find Kelly. Every time he heard of a different school, he ran away to look for her there.

"Finally Mark was sent from the city to our Lake-Side Home because he ran away so much."

That was the end of Mrs. Strong's story about Mark and Kelly.

By this time Mrs. Tandy was crying.

Bill was blinking back tears.

Sammy's eyes looked red.

Kathy was sniffling.

Dave wiped his arm over his eyes.

Then Chief Hemster blew his nose right behind Sammy. It sounded like a brass horn.

Sammy jumped. Then he shouted, "You scared me! I thought a wild elephant had sneaked up on me!"

Everyone had to smile.

Mrs. Strong said, "See what I mean about Mark? Now that my husband and I know his story, we can't stand it.

"We HAVE to help him find Kelly ... and then help both kids if we can."

Dave said, "Listen everyone. Let's not sit around crying! I bet we can find Mark ... today ... before he heads back to the city.

"Then we can ALL help him find Kelly!"

Sammy jumped right up and ran to the door. He shouted, "I'm starting NOW!"

He was halfway out before Bill grabbed him by the pants. "Hold on, Sammy. First we'd better plan this out."

Kathy said, "Yep. Or we might end up having to find you, too!"

Chapter 5: The Bluff Lake Boy Hunt

Chief Hemster said, "My officers are watching for a boy trying to hitch a ride to the city.

"Someone's watching the train station, too.

"We can use the police station as a message center. If you need anything, call there."

Dave said, "If we don't find him by five thirty, let's meet back here."

Bill said, "You know, I don't think Mark would leave for the city without his shoe."

Sammy asked, "Do you think he'd come back for it tonight then?"

Mrs. Tandy said, "We should find him before that."

Mrs. Strong said, "But it seems so hopeless, with all the woods in town to hide in. And so few of us to look!"

Dave said, "Hey! That's it, Mrs. Strong!"

Sammy said, "What's it?"

Dave said, "We can get more help. How many kids can you get from our block, Sammy?"

Sammy shouted, "I see what you mean! I'll get them and go search the ravines with them!"

He zoomed out the door.

Kathy said, "I'll round up all the kids I can find. We can hunt along the bike paths." She ran out, too.

Dave asked, "Are there any people at the home who could help, Mrs. Strong?"

She got up, grabbed her car keys, and said, "You bet. I'll go get them started on the north end of town.

"Then I'll drive to the Garden Club meeting. We gardeners can do the beach and the blocks around it."

Chief Hemster said, "You go to the park, Bill. Find everyone who can help, and hunt all around it.

"I'll go to the junior high and ask the coach to bring the girls' and boys' soccer teams.

"Dave, drive to the high school and ask the coach to bring his teams to the south end of town."

By 4:30 nearly a thousand people were hunting in every yard, woods, garage, store, bush, box, shed, tree, and alley in Bluff Lake.

But by 5:30 the seven tired leaders were back at the house ... without Mark. The others had all gone home.

Dave asked, "Well, do we have any clues at all?"

Chief Hemster said, "Anyone have ANYTHING to report?"

Kathy said, "We know somebody spent a few hours behind the berry bushes on the bike path. The grass was flat, and we found this brown bag. But no Mark."

Everybody looked sad and tired.

Chief Hemster said, "We'd better be going, Ann.

"We have to rest up to hunt again tomorrow."

They said good-bye and the two of them left.

Without saying much, the Woodlanders put together some peanut butter and jelly sandwiches.

They were just finishing up when Mop started barking outside.

Sammy said, "Every time a squirrel

runs near the clubhouse, Mop turns into a nut!"

Bill went out to bring him in. But instead of running over to Bill, Mop ran right up to the clubhouse door.

He hopped and yipped and ran in circles.

Bill heard a thump from inside.

He got scared. He took hold of a board and held it in the air.

He shouted, "All right. Come out of there or I'm coming in after you!"

Slowly the plywood cover over the fire place opening slid aside.

Some one was crawling out backward, feet first.

One foot had a blue shoe on it.

The other had a slipper.

Bill shouted, "Mark!"

Mark said, "Put the board down. I'm not here to fight. I'm here to get some help, if you're not too mad at me."

Bill said, "Mad? No way! Am I glad to see you!"

Mark said, "You ARE? I was afraid you'd hate me.

"I tried to talk to you sooner, but every time I tried to get here, some body walked by.

"It was worse than rush hour in the city. There must have been a thousand people searching around. What were they looking for, anyway?"

Bill started to laugh. He threw an arm around Mark and led him inside.

Mark said, "What's so funny? What WERE they looking for, Bill?"

Bill roared with laughter. He said, "We were all looking for YOU!"

Chapter 6: Mark's Missing Friend

As usual, Sammy was the first to talk.

He shouted, "I don't believe it!"

Kathy said softly, "Wow."

Dave said, "How about that!"

Mrs. Tandy said the first thing that made sense.

She said, "Sit down right here, young man, and eat these cookies while I make you some dinner."

Sammy added, "And let's give one to Mop, the detective dog, as a reward for finding Mark!"

Mrs. Tandy put the cookie jar in front of Mark.

Bill called Chief Hemster, Mrs. Strong, and the Lake-Side Home.

Dave poured a glass of milk and handed it to Mark. He said, "How long have you been out there?"

Mark said, "Only about half an hour. I was going to hide out on the bike path until after school and then come to your clubhouse.

"I wanted to tell Bill I was sorry I picked a fight."

Sammy asked, "Why DID you pick a fight with him, anyway?"

Mark said, "I didn't mean to. When I walked up to him, I was going to ask for help.

"But I got mad instead. I guess I was jealous that Bill had Sammy, and I've lost my friend Kelly. I guess I was mad at everyone.

"I've been watching Bill for two weeks. I kept thinking he'd help me if he could. Then I went and hit him!

"And I was going to tell him about Kelly at noon but he was with the rest of you.

"I sneaked out of Lake-Side last night to say I was sorry, but I chickened out.

"It got so late, I thought I'd sleep in your little house, and talk to him in the morning.

"And I'm sorry about your brick wall.

I bumped into it, hard. And bricks just kept falling down. Someday I'll fix it for you, I promise."

Bill said, "Don't worry. We can put that wall up again together."

Mark went on. "So, anyway, I missed you after school, Bill.

"There were mobs of kids around. Even in your yard.

"I was afraid someone might see me, and turn me in to the home before I could talk to you."

Kathy said, "We had the whole town looking for you."

Mark said, "Why? Because I hit Bill? And messed up your brick walls?"

Sammy blabbed out, "Because Mrs. Strong told us about you and Kelly, that's why. And WE are going to help you find her!"

Mark said, "I just know she ran away

again to look for me."

Dave said, "Well, we can start looking for HER! It's Saturday tomorrow, no school, so we can head for the city."

Bill said, "Let's make a list of places she might be."

Kathy said, "I'll get Mark's shoe first. Then we can start."

Mark slipped his foot into the shoe. Now every one crowded around him.

Mark looked around at everyone. He said, "I ... I never had so many friends ... I want ... you're being so nice to me ..."

All of a sudden he put his head down on his arms.

He started crying his heart out!

Just then Chief Hemster drove up.

Then Dr. and Mrs. Strong came to the door.

There was a lot of hugging when the Strongs saw Mark.

But Dr. Strong had some bad news for him.

He said, "Today I phoned your case-workers to find out where Kelly was. I thought they might tell me.

"They said they wanted to help us, but it's too late. Kelly ran away from her last foster home a month ago.

"No one knows where she is, Mark. And her foot was giving her a bad time again."

Chief Hemster said, "Tomorrow's my day off. If it's OK with everyone, I'll head up a city hunt for Kelly."

Dave said, "That would be great, Chief."

Chief Hemster said, "We can take my police car and your car, Dave.

"Mark can ride with you to tell you where to go. Dr. Strong and Sammy can ride with you, too. I'll take the others."

Mrs. Tandy said, "Where should we start to look?"

Bill said, "Let's figure it out right now."

Mark came up with this list:

our old apartment house
two libraries
stores we used
places we asked for work
the park
the plant house in the park

Chief Hemster asked Mark to add these notes to the list:

call city police
call TV stations
call newspapers

The next morning everyone was ready. Chief Hemster called the city police. They promised to help hunt for Kelly.

The newspapers and TV stations said they would run the story of the search, too.

So the Bluff Lake detectives piled into the cars.

Then Chief Hemster said, "Wait! Where's Becky?"

They looked up and saw Mrs. Tandy. She was pushing out of the front door with two shopping bags.

Mrs. Tandy smiled. She said, "I made sandwiches, in case we can't stop for lunch!"

Sammy said, "Now we are REALLY ready for the great city hunt!"

Chapter 7: The Hunt Begins

By the time they got to the city it was 10:00 in the morning.

Mark had them stop in front of an old building.

He ran up to the front door. Sammy, Bill, and Kathy followed right behind him.

Sammy exclaimed, "Holy cats! Look! Almost every window is broken. And the ones on the first floor have boards over them.

"Did you really live here, Mark?"

Mark said, "Yep. And we were lucky we could."

Mark knocked five times on the cracked door. Then he kicked twice and knocked five times again.

They waited.

At first it seemed as if no one would answer.

Then they heard some un-even foot steps inside.

The door opened a crack.

A thin, worried old face peeked out at them.

Then the door flew open.

A wrinkled old man with a cast and crutches stood inside.

His face broke into an ear-to-ear smile when he saw Mark.

He reached forward to grab his arm. He cried, "Mark! Is it really you?"

He pulled the boy to him. "Come on in! I haven't heard our secret knock in so long!

"I've sure missed you. I just about gave up on you. I never did think I'd see you kids again.

"Is Kelly's foot healed?"

Then the old man took a good look at Sammy, Bill, and Kathy. He asked, "Who are these young folks?"

He looked at the two cars at the curb. He saw Chief Hemster getting out of the police car.

He asked, "What's that police officer here for ... you kids in bad trouble?"

Mark said, "No, I think I'm finally getting out of trouble, Cappy. These are all my friends."

He pointed to the Strongs standing near the curb.

He said, "The Strongs want to give Kelly and me a home with them. But Kelly ran away from another foster home, and now no one knows where she is."

Mark pointed to the crutches. He said, "What's wrong with you, Cappy? Why the cast?"

Cappy said, "Broke my leg when a floorboard in the hall came loose. Tripped before I saw it. Almost healed now, though."

The others came over from the cars.

Mark said, "This is Cappy. He's the one who gave me and Kelly a place to live."

Everyone shook his hand.

Chief Hemster said, "Have you seen Kelly Evans since she and Mark left that day for the hospital?"

Cappy said, "No. She's a real sweetheart. Wish I did have some news of her.

"But come inside. Maybe I can help. Might have a clue."

Cappy swung his leg with its heavy cast. He led them into the front hall.

The tile was dirty and cracked.

The white marble floor had drips of paint and stains all over it.

Then Cappy led them down a dark gray hall with a wooden floor.

Scraps of dirty carpet pad were stuck to it.

Old bent tacks stuck out of it.

A board stuck up.

Cappy said, "Here's where I tripped. Watch out. Can't fix it until I'm out of the cast."

Sammy whispered to Bill, "Yuck! If I were a bug, I'd be living in this hall.

"I'll never complain about cleaning up my room again! I don't want it to end up looking like this!"

Bill whispered back, "Too bad. It already does."

Sammy made his killer-snake face at him.

They went on down the hall. There were no light bulbs on the ceiling. There were holes in the plaster, and some doors missing.

At last Cappy stopped in front of a closed door.

He said, "Here's my apartment!" and opened it.

They saw a clean, cozy room. It had a neat bed with a red cover, and short red curtains.

It had a yellow table with three chairs, a bright blue dresser, a rocking chair, and book shelves.

Cappy said, "Please sit down." He seated himself in his rocker with his broken leg sticking forward.

The others sat around him on the bed and chairs.

Cappy went on talking. "Something happened about two weeks ago that set me thinking about you kids, Mark."

Chief Hemster said, "What was it?"

Cappy said, "Heard some noise late one night. Someone moving around outside.

"Then some rocks landed on the floor in the room above this one.

"I was thinking it was wild kids again, trying to break more glass.

"You know, even after a window's broken, there's still glass left around the sides.

"I don't mind saying I was scared. Even called the cops.

"They kept an eye out for a few nights. No more rocks, so they left."

Sammy said, "Wow! I'd be scared, too, hearing glass break and rocks fall right above me.

"When you went up, was it a big mess?"

Cappy said, "Well, see, I couldn't go up to check because of my leg. But here's the funny part ..."

Mark said, "What, Cappy?"

Cappy said, "When I began to think it over, I didn't remember hearing any glass break. None at all."

Mrs. Tandy said, "My, they must have had terrible aim."

Dr. Strong said, "Yes, you'd think they'd hit the glass that was left at least once, if they tried."

Cappy said, "That's just it! After a few days it came to me. Whoever threw the rocks didn't WANT to break any glass!"

Sammy said, "Why would somebody throw rocks in the window, anyway?

"Wouldn't they worry about waking you up?"

Suddenly Dave shouted, "KELLY! It must have been Kelly!

"TRYING to wake you up, Cappy!

"Afraid she'd be caught by the police if

she knocked on the door or broke some glass."

Cappy nodded. "Just what I've been thinking lately. Been thinking something else, too.

"What if Kelly tied a message to one of those rocks? But like I said, with this leg I can't go up to look. Why don't you?"

Bill and Sammy grabbed Dave's wheelchair.

In a second, everyone was dashing to the second floor.

Chapter 8:
The *Robinson Crusoe* Clue

They ran to the room above Cappy's.

Glass and rocks lay all over the floor.

They looked around.

Bill darted over to a corner and said, "What's this!"

He held up a rock. It was wrapped in paper, with a rubber band to keep the paper in place.

Sammy yelled, "Wow! It's from Kelly, I know it is!"

Mrs. Tandy said, "Look at this!" She had a rock, too.

Mark found one, too, and opened it up. The paper said

They found eight rocks, all with the same note on them.

Mark said, "It's Kelly's writing, all right."

Dave asked, "Do you know what it means, Mark?"

He said, "I wish I did. Let's go show Cappy and try to figure it out."

They headed downstairs.

They showed Cappy what they had found.

Cappy said, "How about that. A message from little Kelly."

Kathy asked, "Why would Kelly write down the name of an old book?"

Sammy said, "Maybe she's living on an island, like that guy Robinson Crusoe."

Mrs. Tandy asked, "Why did she write a code message? Why couldn't she just say where she was?"

Dr. Strong said, "She must have been

afraid she'd be picked up by the police, and never find Mark."

Bill asked, "Mark, does that December date mean anything to you or Kelly?"

Mark shook his head. "Not that I can think of."

Dave said, "Well, it looks like all we have to go on for sure is the book, *Robinson Crusoe*. We'd better get hold of a copy."

Mark said, "The nearest library is just two blocks away. We can get it there."

Cappy said, "Wait. I'll lock up. I'm going with you."

They drove to the library. It was in an old store building.

PUBLIC LIBRARY was painted on the window.

Over the door it said BRANCH 5.

The outside of the library was run-down, but the inside was cheerful. Clean tables, chairs, and colorful books filled the room.

Chief Hemster nodded to the librarian.

Mark led the way to the right shelf. He said, "Here's *Robinson Crusoe.*"

Sammy said, "Here's another one. It's bigger and has bigger printing. I bet it's easier to read, too."

They took both books to a table. They began flipping through the pages.

Suddenly Dave said, "Wait a minute!"

His voice was so loud the librarian looked up and said, "Shh ..."

Dave whispered, "Look at this! There's a date on this page!"

It said September 30, 1659.

Mark whispered, "Hey, I remember now. There are tons of dates in this book. Quick, see what Robinson Crusoe wrote on the date from Kelly's note."

They quickly found December 20, line one.

Kathy read out loud, "Now I carried everything into the ..."

Mrs. Strong read the other copy. "Now I carried everything into the cave and ..."

Dr. Strong said, "Every printing of this book might not be spaced the same. But

Kelly must have meant some cave.

"Quick, look for the next clue."

They found page 131, line 3.

Sammy read aloud, "That I was king and lord of all this country ..."

Mrs. Tandy read from the other copy. It said, " ... very heavy."

Cappy asked, "Is this making any sense to anybody?"

Mrs. Tandy said, "Wait. Just a minute. What if we don't have the right copy of *Robinson Crusoe?*"

Bill said, "That's it! Let me see Kelly's note! Look. It says 'Ill. N.P.,' whatever that means."

Kathy asked, "Could 'Ill. N.P.' mean the book was illustrated by a person whose first and last names begin with an N and a P?

"And what does that last clue, 'PLB 6' mean?"

Dave said, "Come here, Kathy."

She followed him over to the desk.

Dave said to the librarian, "Please, we need your help. We have to find out what these clues mean."

Kathy said, "A missing girl left them for us, and we have to find her. Do you know an 'N. P.' who illustrated a *Robinson Crusoe?"*

Dave showed the piece of paper to the librarian.

She said, "Why, there is a copy of

Robinson Crusoe with pictures by Noel Pocock. But we don't have it.

"The 'PLB 6' on this note must mean Public Library Branch 6. Maybe they have this copy. I'll phone them for you."

After she called, she said, "Yes. They have it at Branch 6, in the park."

Dave and Kathy hurried back to the table. They told everyone what the clues meant.

They all jumped up from the table and dashed to the door.

Kathy whispered to the librarian, "Thanks! Thank you so much!" as the ten of them clattered out with Dave's wheelchair.

This time the librarian didn't say "Shh..." to them.

She called softly, "Good luck!"

They jumped into the cars so fast that Mark nearly landed on Kathy's lap.

Chapter 9: Searching the Park

They rushed into Public Library Branch 6, at the end of the park.

They took out the right *Robinson Crusoe* book at last. They all stood around it like players in a football huddle.

Mrs. Tandy said, "OK. We know there's a cave. So what's the third clue?"

Mark read aloud from page 131, line 3, "... sweet, adorned with flowers, and full of very fine woods."

He said, "Well, that can't mean the plant house.

"It has beautiful flowers, all right, but no cave. And almost no trees. You couldn't call it a woods. That only leaves the park."

Dr. Strong cried, "That's it, then! It MUST mean there's a cave in the park, with flowers near it, and woods all around. Let's go!"

Sammy said, "Hey, I know we have to find Kelly, but I'm too hungry to hunt. Where are those sandwiches?"

He ran back to the car and got them.

Chief Hemster said, "We can eat while

we hunt in the park. There are ten of us, so we can work in five pairs. Where do we start, Mark?"

Mark said, "Well, this park is huge. Kelly and I spent a lot of time here. But we never looked for a cave.

"It has flowers and woods everywhere. I have no idea where to start."

Chief Hemster said, "Then let's divide the park into five strips. Each pair of us will search a strip."

Mark drew the plan on paper.

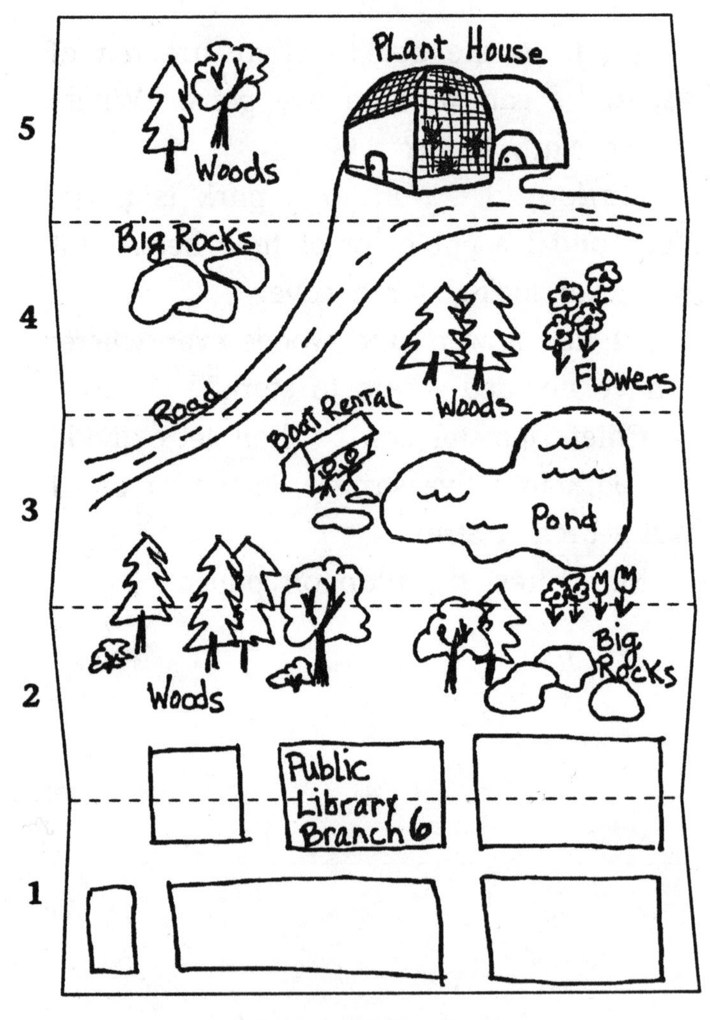

Map of City Park

Chief Hemster said, "Dave, you go with Sammy.

"Ann, you come with me.

"Kathy, you go with Dr. Strong.

"Cappy, you go with Mark."

He turned to Mrs. Tandy. He said, "Becky, that leaves you and Bill. If we don't find Kelly sooner, we will meet back here at five."

"Stay with your partners!" Bill called as they started off.

At 5:00, the ten tired hunters met in front of the library.

They hadn't found a thing.

They were hungry.

They were wet with sweat.

They were dirty.

They were scratched.

They had bug bites.

Sammy said, "Dave and I called

'KELLY' until our lungs were coming loose. But we've come up with ZERO!"

Mark said, "And Cappy and I asked every person we saw about a cave. No one knows about a cave, not even park workers."

The others said, "We asked, too."

Bill said, "We walked into every woods and looked behind every huge rock."

The others said, "We did, too."

Dr. Strong said, "Kathy and I even rented a paddleboat ... the kind you pedal like a bike.

"We went all over the pond looking for caves on the sides. Not a thing but cattails and bushes."

Sammy cried, "You lucky duck, Kathy! Why didn't you take me? I would have put a safety pin on a string and caught us some fish.

"I'm as hungry as a hippo and as low as a mud puddle!"

Chief Hemster said, "We all are. Right now let's go get dinner. Then we can take Cappy home and get some sleep at a motel.

"We can begin again early tomorrow."

Dr. Strong put an arm around Mark. He said, "Don't feel too bad, my boy. We will find her."

Dave said, "As soon as we have some food and some sleep, we will think of something, Mark."

Mrs. Tandy said, "We can call the newspapers and TV stations and police tonight and see what they've found."

Mark smiled a bright smile at his friends.

But inside he was plenty worried.

And the Woodlanders were, too.

Chapter 10: Flowers and Very Fine Woods

The next morning they picked up Cappy.

They went out for a pancake breakfast.

As they ate, Dave looked over Mark's list of places to hunt.

Dave said, "It looks like all that's left to search are the stores and the plant house in the park."

Chief Hemster said, "We might as well start with the stores. I noticed the plant house is closed mornings."

Sammy said, "We'd better get plenty of energy stored up for the hunt. Pass the syrup, please, and the eggs."

Mark said, "Let's start with the stores near the park. I can tell you which ones Kelly might have gone into."

The first block had four stores on it that Kelly might try. Mark, Bill, and Kathy went inside one.

Mark went up to the teen-age boy behind the counter.

He said, "I'm looking for my friend. Has a skinny eleven-year-old girl with freckles been in lately?"

The boy asked in a mean voice,

"What will you pay me if I tell you?"

Kathy said, "Come on! This girl is lost!"

The boy said, "So what?"

Mark said, "Let me talk to your boss, then."

The boy said, "Slip me a couple of bucks and I'll go get him."

Then Bill said in a loud voice, "Get your boss out here, fast."

The boy took one look at Bill's angry face. Suddenly he ran to the back of the store.

They heard him call, "Boss! Mr. East!"

In a minute the boy came back with his boss.

Mr. East looked at Mark and asked, "What can I do for you? Say, didn't you used to come in here with your sister?"

Mark said, "Yes, sir, but she isn't exactly my sister. She's my best friend, Kelly Evans. I'm Mark Witt."

Mr. East said, "I remember you two asking for jobs months ago. But I didn't need anyone.

"Hey, come to think of it, your friend was here just about two weeks ago ... looking for work."

Mark gasped, "Kelly was here!"

Questions came spilling out of him.

"How was she?

"Was she all right?

"Did she look like she's getting enough to eat?

"Was she walking OK?

"Did she say where she was going?

"Did she say anything about me?

"Did she have any money?

"Which way did she go when she left here?

"Why—"

Mr East smiled and said, "Whoa! Let me tell you what I can. She didn't look too good.

"She was limping, and thin and pale. I still had my old helper then, so I didn't hire her. I wish I had now."

Mark felt heart-sick.

He asked softly, "Do you at least know where she went?"

Mr. East said, "Well, no. But I made her take two loaves of bread with her and some cold meat and a few apples. I told her I had ordered too much. I sure hope you find her."

Mark said, "We've GOT to find her! In case she turns up, here's our phone number at the motel.

"And thanks for feeding her, sir."

Kathy said, "And here's our phone number where we live.

"Tell her Mark is looking everywhere for her.

"Tell her everything will be all right.

"And thank you."

The three of them hurried outside.

The others were waiting there for them ... everyone but Sammy.

Kathy said, "Hooray! Kelly is around here somewhere ... right under our noses!"

Suddenly Sammy raced up. He said, "Hey! Look! Where did I put that stupid thing! Oh, here it is. No, that's not it!"

He was twisting and turning, and patting all his pockets.

Then he pulled out all the junk in them: a pencil, a writing pad, marbles, his wallet, a compass, and a few rubber bands.

At last he found a folded piece of paper.

He shouted, "Look at this! It was taped up in a store window.

"It says here they're having a show at the plant house!"

He showed them the paper.

It said this:

A show of
Very Fine Woods
for
Furniture Making

Everyone stared at him.

Then Bill shouted, "A show of very fine woods! At the plant house! That makes the plant house almost fit the *Robinson Crusoe* clues!

"'A cave ... sweet, adorned with flowers and full of very fine woods!' The only thing missing is the cave!"

Mrs. Strong was hugging Sammy.

Kathy, Chief Hemster, and Dr. Strong were patting his back.

Mrs. Tandy was kissing him.

Bill grabbed him and hugged him.

Then they ran for the cars.

As they got in, Dave said, "That settles it! Somewhere in that plant house, there's GOT to be a cave. And we WILL find it. And that's where Kelly is!"

Chapter 11: The Cave

They went back to the park.

They rushed to the plant house.

The Woodlanders and their friends hurried to the big glass doors. But the chief was right. They were locked.

A sign said

OPEN DAILY, 12:00 TO 5:00 P.M.

It was only 10:00.

Chief Hemster ran back to his car.

Sammy went with him. He said, "Oh, boy! I bet you're getting your bullets to shoot off the lock! Right?"

The chief snorted. He said, "Wrong! Do you think I'd put everyone in danger? Why, there'd be broken glass everywhere!"

Sammy said, "Then you're going to bash it in carefully with your club! Right?"

Chief Hemster laughed. "No, Sammy. Nothing so wild." He turned on his two-way car radio and called the city police.

They called the keeper of the plant house.

In ten minutes a man drove up.

Chief Hemster said, "Thanks for

coming so fast! We think a missing girl is locked up inside the plant house!"

The man jumped out of the car. He ran to the door and un-locked it.

They all ran with him into a large hallway. It was empty except for a few benches.

Then he led them into a hot, damp room full of plants and flowers. The round ceiling was a big dome of steel and glass.

Plants grew everywhere ...
on piles of rocks
in pots on benches
across the dirt floor
in small indoor ponds
... and from the walls.

Mark called out, "Kelly? Kelly, are you here?"

He listened. Everyone stood as still as a rock and listened.

Even Sammy.

"Kelly!" Mark called again. "It's Mark! Are you in here, Kelly?"

The glass dome above them sent back an echo, but that was all.

Mark said, "Quick, tell me. Which room has a cave in it?"

The keeper of the plant house said, "A cave? Why, there's no cave in the plant house. And I would know! I've worked here for twenty years!"

Chief Hemster said, "But there's got to be a cave."

The man said, "Nope. Sorry. Still, cave or no cave, I'll help you look for the lost girl.

"My name's Rick Yamada. I've got the keys for every room and every storage space right here."

He held up a heavy steel ring, much bigger than a bracelet. It had about thirty keys on it.

Mr. Yamada found the keys to the storage closets in the room they were in.

Chief Hemster said, "Cappy and Bill, check one closet. Dr. Strong and Sammy, check out the other. We will search the rest of the room."

Mr. Yamada warned, "Be careful not to step on even the smallest plant. Many of these are very rare."

They searched under every bush, and

around every bunch of flowerpots, and behind every rock pile.

At last they had searched every inch of the first room.

The room was so hot they were all sweating.

Sammy wiped his head. He said, "Wow. A rare plant might love this room, or a frog, even.

"But not me! It's too hot and damp. Let's get out of here before we drip to death!"

They moved along to the next room. It was cool and dry, and HUGE.

The room had stone walls and a round stone ceiling. One wall had a giant window cut in it.

A set of shelves that went up like steps filled one side. They looked like bleachers at a baseball game. Pots of flowers covered every inch of them.

Tables stood at one end of the room.

They began calling, "Kelly! Kelly! Are you here?"

But no one answered.

Kathy said, "Well, maybe she's not here. But if I were Kelly, I would've chosen this room to hide in. It's dry and nice in here ... like a cool cave."

"A CAVE!" shouted Dave and Bill and Mark all at once.

Bill shouted, "We don't have to look for a cave IN a room.

"This whole room is a big cave!

It has stone walls, and a stone roof—"

Chief Hemster said, "And look at what's on these tables!

"Wood squares!

"They're marked 'Fine Woods for Furniture Making!'"

Dave said, "This room fits the whole clue! 'A cave ... sweet, adorned with flowers and full of very fine woods.' Kelly MUST be here somewhere!"

Mark said, "But if she IS here, and she's not answering, then something must be wrong with her."

Bill said, "Maybe she's just scared of all these people, and doesn't know if it's safe."

Sammy said, "Then we have to look for her!

"Hey! The table covers go all the way to the floor. I'll bet you she's hiding under one of them."

They all started calling Kelly's name again, but got no answer.

Kathy ran to a table and lifted its cover. Under it were big boxes that the rare woods had been packed in.

But Kelly wasn't there.

The Woodlanders moved every box and looked again.

At last Mark said quietly, "I was so sure we'd find her in here."

Dave said, "Me, too. But there are lots of other rooms to search."

Just then Bill whispered to Sammy, "Hey, Sammy, remember when Dad used to take us to football games?

"How we used to hide under the bleachers? Well, do you think Kelly—?"

He never got to finish.

Sammy darted over to the bleachers. He started taking flowerpots off one of the rows of steps.

Mr. Yamada called, "Wait a minute, you little imp! Don't mess up that display!"

But the others saw what Sammy was up to. They ran over to the bleachers and began taking pots off, too.

Mr. Yamada kept saying, "Oh, no. Oh, dear me."

Then Sammy stuck his head into the space they had made.

He yelped, "I see something in there!"

He crawled inside.

Mark, Kathy, Bill, and Mrs. Tandy followed him in.

The others heard Mark say, "Kelly. Kelly, it's me. Wake up."

Kathy called out, "Dr. Strong, she's here! But there's something wrong with her! She won't wake up!"

Bill added, "And she feels all hot when you touch her."

Sammy shouted, "And she's as limp as a noodle! NOW what do we do?"

Chapter 12: The Hospital

Dr. Strong called in to them, "Mr. Yamada and I will rig up a stretcher.

"Can you lift Kelly out to us?

"You have to keep her perfectly flat.

"We don't know what's wrong with her yet."

They worked for a few minutes. Then they handed the stretcher under the bleachers.

Mrs. Tandy said, "Can you pick her up, kids, while I hold her head?"

Bill said, "Sure. Sammy, you and Mark take that side. Kathy and I will take this side. All together now, LIFT."

They handed the stretcher through the opening.

With careful hands, Chief Hemster, the Strongs, Dave, and Mr. Yamada lifted the stretcher out. They put it gently down on the floor.

Chief Hemster said, "Why, she's as light as a feather. Poor girl, she's so thin."

Mrs. Tandy said, "One of her feet is all wrapped with rags. Is that the one she hurt before, Mark?"

Mark nodded. His eyes were full of tears. He said, "I wish I had found her weeks ago."

The doctor gave some orders. He said, "Mr. Yamada, please get us some clean water.

"Bill, get my bag from the car.

"Chief, call an ambulance."

Dr. Strong felt Kelly's head.

He said, "She's hot and dry. She has a fever. Her leg looks badly infected and swollen.

"But she doesn't seem to have any broken bones.

"Let's get my bag open, and I'll listen to her heart and breathing."

Sammy poked Bill and whispered, "You think she will be OK?"

Bill patted his younger brother's arm.

He said, "At least she has a chance, Sammy. Finding her may have saved her life, you little imp."

Sammy socked Bill on the arm.

Bill said, "Hey, don't hit me! That's what Mr. Yamada called you when you took down his flower pots!"

Sammy said, "Well, you're the one who thought of looking under the bleachers. You're the real hero, Bill!"

Mr. Yamada came out of a storage space with a glass of water and a pail.

Kathy, Mark, and Dr. Strong held Kelly up a little. The doctor wanted her to get just a taste of water.

Mark said, "Here, Kelly. Drink this. It's me, Mark. Oh, please, Kelly, wake up."

Mark dripped a little water between her dry lips.

Mark went on. "Please wake up, Kelly. You're OK now. I'm going to take care of you. Kelly, can you hear me?"

Dr. Strong said, "Keep talking to her.

The sound of your voice may be just what she needs. Maybe it will bring her out of this."

He said to his wife, "Here, Ann. Cool her down with these gauze pads dipped in that pail.

"Do her wrists and hands."

Dave asked, "Want me to do her ankles?"

Dr. Strong said, "Fine. I'm going to give her some anti-biotic shots to start fighting that infection."

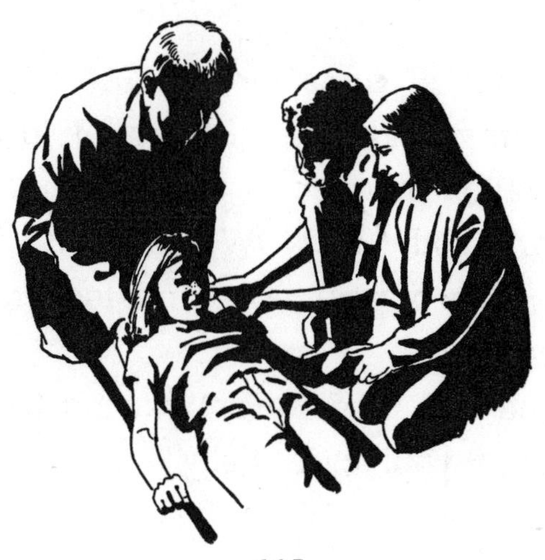

Mrs. Strong cooled and patted Kelly's hands.

She whispered, "Only let Kelly live, and I'll bring up both of these kids. They'll never be homeless again."

Dr. Strong said, "Give her another sip of water, Mark.

"I think ... I think ... did you see her move her lips a tiny bit? Did her throat move? Did she swallow?"

Mark said, "I think so! Come on, Kelly! Wake up and look at me. It's me. It's Mark.

"We've all come for you."

Sammy said, "Hey, I think I just saw her eyelids move!"

Mark said, "I KNOW I did! It's Mark, Kelly! Open your eyes and look at me. I found you.

"And this time we are staying together. Just open your eyes, Kelly."

Mrs. Strong's kind voice shook, but she said, "Kelly, honey, open your eyes for Mark. Please open your eyes."

Slowly Kelly's eyelids lifted. She looked at the faces above her. Her pale lips turned up in a weak smile.

She whispered, "Mark! I knew you'd come for me."

Then she fainted away.

They heard the siren of a far-off ambulance.

Then they heard the ambulance driving up.

Bill and Chief Hemster ran to the front doors. They came back with the medics.

The medics loaded Kelly into the ambulance. Dr. Strong and Mark rode with her to the hospital.

Everyone else jumped into the cars. With sirens screaming, the ambulance raced to the hospital.

In a few minutes, Kelly was in the emergency room.

Nurses and doctors were working to save her.

The others all sat in the waiting room. Dr. Strong came out to them.

Mark said, "Is she OK? Can I go in there now?"

Dr. Strong said, "She's in trouble, but I think she's going to make it."

Mrs. Tandy said, "Thank goodness!" She gave Mark a hug.

Bill asked, "How long will she have to be in the hospital?"

Dr. Strong said, "I think she could be in this hospital for at least a week. Then we can take her to our hospital in Bluff Lake.

"She may have to stay there even longer. We are going to clear up her leg infection for good!"

Sammy said, "Hey, Dr. Strong, I think Mark should skip school and stay down here. Just until Kelly can come to Bluff Lake!"

Dr. Strong said, "Sammy, were you listening in on my brain?

"In fact, I just arranged that with the hospital.

"Mark, you can sleep here, and Ann and I will stay at the motel."

He added, "I called the boys' home, and they said it would be fine."

Mark said, "Good, because I'm never leaving Kelly again."

Sammy said, "Come to think of it, I better stay out of school for a while, too. I'd sure feel a lot better ... and I bet my teacher would feel like a million dollars!"

They all laughed.

Kathy said, "No, Sammy. Really, she'd probably miss you."

Sammy said, "Thanks, Kathy. But you're my sister. You HAVE to like me!"

Chief Hemster said, "Well, looks to me like we should get everybody home.

"Cappy? Mr. Yamada? We all want to thank you two."

Cappy said, "Hey, anything for those kids."

Mr. Yamada said, "I'm just glad we found her!"

They took Cappy home, and Mr. Yamada back to his car at the plant house.

Then the Woodlanders and Chief Hemster headed back to Bluff Lake.

They could hardly wait for Mark and Kelly to come home.

Chapter 13: The New Family

It took a week to get Kelly well enough to sit up a little.

Then Dr. Strong had her taken by ambulance to the Bluff Lake Hospital.

Her fever had made her forget everything that happened the day they found her.

She didn't remember the Woodland family, Chief Hemster, or the Strongs.

She didn't even remember talking to Mark.

Now they all sat with her in the hospital sun room.

They told her everything about the great city hunt.

Kelly told them all about the last three months of her life.

She had been placed in a new foster home as soon as the cut on her foot was better.

She said, "I kept asking my new foster parents about Mark. They tried to find out for me, but the caseworker wasn't allowed to tell.

"My foot was still hurting, but just a

little. So I sneaked away one night and started looking for Mark."

Sammy asked, "Where did you go?"

She said, "Nowhere, really. I lived on the street the way Mark and I used to.

"I looked for jobs. Every morning I waited near a different school, looking for Mark."

Dave asked, "Why didn't you try to find Cappy's place?"

Kelly said, "I didn't go back at first because I was afraid they'd be looking for me in the old places."

Mrs. Tandy asked, "How did you stay warm at night?"

Kelly said, "Well, at first, when it was still pretty warm out, I'd lie down in a park on thick newspaper.

"Mark told me how the air between the papers keeps you warm.

"Newspaper makes a good cover, too.

So I'd put parts of it over me and tuck it in on the sides."

Kathy asked, "What about when it got colder out?"

Kelly said, "That's when I remembered how warm the plant house was. Mark and I used to go there sometimes when we got cold.

"So when I got there I came up with this plan.

"It was about half an hour before they locked the doors inside.

"I looked until I found a big bushy plant. Then, when no one was near me, I slid in back of it."

Sammy said, "Did you sleep in the same place every day?"

She said, "I sure didn't. There was a big anthill near that bush, and I found it the very first night.

"No, it found me!

"I had to take off my clothes and shake all the ants out. I was scratching myself for DAYS.

"Anyway, I found other places to hide. In about two weeks, some workers set up the bleachers and flowerpots.

"I moved in under them.

"It was dark and cool there, so I took newspapers in.

"There's a good place at the end near the wall to get in and out. I only had to move two pots."

Chief Hemster said, "And all that time, Mark was looking for you!"

Kelly said, "By then, my foot was really sore again. I think because I didn't clean it off like I should have."

Dave said, "How could you have?"

Kelly said, "Anyway, I had an awful cold. And I was so tired all the time. Pretty soon I knew I HAD to get a message to Cappy.

"I hoped he'd get it to Mark."

Mrs. Tandy said, "So that's why you took the risk and went to Cappy's that night."

Kelly nodded. "Yep. Then a day before you found me, I ate up my last food. I felt so sick, I couldn't even go for water.

"I bet I'd have died if you hadn't come for me."

Mrs. Strong said, "Bless your heart, child,

don't even say that! I can't stand it.

"You think about other things, like getting well and coming home to us!"

That afternoon Ann Strong heard the doorbell ring. She opened the door.

There stood Sammy, Mrs. Tandy, Kathy, Dave, and Bill.

Mrs. Strong said, "Why, hello, you dears! Come right in and sit down."

Sammy said, "We can come right in, but we won't sit down."

Kathy said, "We were thinking about how much work you'll have to do to get ready for a new family. So we drove over to help!"

Mrs. Strong said, "Well, thank you! I would have had trouble getting ready in time. But with your help I can do it."

So the Woodlanders hammered and sawed and painted and sewed after school

every day for two weeks.

Mark spent most of his after-school time with Kelly in the hospital.

Then one Friday Dr. Strong came to tell them the news.

Kelly was much better.

She still had to stay in bed, but she was coming home tomorrow.

The next morning Dr. Strong and Mark helped Kelly into the house. Chief Hemster was there, too. And the Woodlanders.

Mrs. Strong hugged Mark and Kelly tight, and said, "Home at last."

Everyone went upstairs. They all helped Kelly into bed.

Mrs. Strong, Bill, Mrs. Tandy, Kathy, and the doctor went down again. This time they came upstairs with a party!

They brought hats made from newspapers, paper plates, and a huge pizza.

Last came Mrs. Tandy with a giant plate of oatmeal cookies.

Everyone clapped and cheered.

Then Dr. Strong said, "Welcome home at last! And I want to tell everyone that the adoption papers came today.

"We have the OK to go ahead and adopt Mark and Kelly!"

The Woodlanders and their friends cheered even louder.

The two lost runaways had been found for good.